PROJECT PEEP

Read the rest of the books in the
FRIENDSHIP GARDEN
series:

Green Thumbs-Up!

Pumpkin Spice

And coming soon

Sweet Peas and Honeybees

the FRIENDSHIP garden

PROJECT PEEP

by Jenny Meyerhoff
illustrated by Éva Chatelain

ALADDIN
New York London Toronto Sydney New Delhi

ALADDIN

An imprint of Simon & Schuster Children's Publishing Division
1230 Avenue of the Americas, New York, NY 10020
This Aladdin hardcover edition January 2016
Text copyright © 2016 by Simon & Schuster, Inc.
Illustrations copyright © 2016 by Éva Chatelain
Also available in an Aladdin paperback edition.
For information about special discounts for bulk purchases, please contact Simon & Schuster Special Sales at 1-866-506-1949 or business@simonandschuster.com.
The Simon & Schuster Speakers Bureau can bring authors to your live event. For more information or to book an event contact the Simon & Schuster Speakers Bureau at 1-866-248-3049 or visit our website at www.simonspeakers.com.
Book designed by Laura Lyn DiSiena
The text of this book was set in Century Expanded LT Std.
Manufactured in the United States of America 1215 FFG
10 9 8 7 6 5 4 3 2 1
Library of Congress Control Number 2015955335
ISBN 978-1-4814-3914-5 (hc)
ISBN 978-1-4814-3913-8 (pbk)
ISBN 978-1-4814-3915-2 (eBook)

For Adam

PROJECT PEEP

CONTENTS

CHAPTER 1

CHICKEN SCHOOL

Anna Fincher was having a hard time paying attention to her teacher, Mr. Hoffman. It wasn't because he was being boring. In fact, he was telling her third-grade class about a party!

For the past two months, Anna's class had watched chicken eggs develop in an incubator. Then they'd seen the eggs hatch and they'd taken care of the baby chicks as they grew.

"Friday will be our last day with the chicks in this classroom," Mr. Hoffman told his students. "We will have a party to say good-bye."

All of Anna's classmates groaned. Anna groaned too, but not because of the chicks. She had something else on her mind: Kaya's birthday. She didn't have time to worry about chicks. She needed to think of a present for Kaya.

In just one week Anna's friend Kaya would be turning nine years old, and Anna wanted to get her the best birthday present E-V-E-R. But that was the problem—Anna didn't know what Kaya would want most of all.

New gel pens? Kaya loved to draw and paint.

Rainbow tights? Anna was wearing tights

with suns and moons on them. Maybe Kaya would like a pair too.

Maybe she should get Kaya a squirting bow tie? No, that would be a better present for their friend Reed. He loved practical jokes.

"I'm so sad," Kaya whispered to Anna. "How will we survive without seeing Lemondrop, Chicken Little, Fluff, and Feather? They're my friends, and now they are going to be gone." She sighed.

Anna nodded. She knew what it was like to say good-bye to friends. When she lived in Rosendale, New York, she'd had two best friends, Haley and Lauren. But since Anna had moved to Chicago eight months ago, they hadn't kept in touch the way she'd thought they would. Even though Anna still wore the purple BFF bracelet they'd made, Anna wasn't sure they still counted as *best* friends.

And if they didn't, then Anna didn't have a best friend anymore.

Kaya tapped Anna's shoulder. "You know what the worst part is? I have to say good-bye on my birthday."

"That's the opposite of a birthday present." Anna frowned. "It's a birthday punishment."

When Anna had first moved to Chicago, Kaya had been Anna's first friend. Kaya had even helped Anna start the Friendship Garden, their school's gardening club. Anna wanted to give Kaya something she would never forget. If the present was good enough, maybe Kaya would realize they should be best friends.

Anna really *did* know the perfect present for Kaya. She just couldn't get it for her. Kaya wanted a pet more than anything, but her parents were too busy running their frozen yogurt shop to help take care of one.

The bell rang and all of Anna's classmates got up to collect their belongings, but Anna, Kaya, and Reed went over to Chicken School. That was what Anna had nicknamed the corner of the classroom where Mr. Hoffman had set up the chickens. Anna loved nicknaming things.

Chicken School had a big glass tank, like an aquarium, lined with wood shavings on the bottom. Dishes for food and water sat in one corner of the tank. There was a big light hooked onto the top to keep the chicks warm. Kaya sat right in front of the chicks and began to coo at them. Reed sat next to her.

To the left of the tank was a small plastic

wading pool, the kind that Anna used to splash in when she was little. It was just the right size for the chickens to play in now that they weren't teeny tiny anymore.

Anna sat down on the side of the empty pool. She couldn't believe how much the chicks had grown since they'd been in her classroom. They'd started out the size of tennis balls and now they were practically as big as footballs.

"Hi, Feather," Kaya sang, picking up the biggest one and nuzzling her cheek against its head. "You are such a good little chickie!"

Kaya put Feather in the pool and he looked up at her like she was his mama hen. All the chicks liked Kaya best of anyone in their class. She was the perfect mix of gentle and playful. One by one, she picked up each of the four birds and set them in the pool. They made

tiny peeping noises as they scurried around, bumping into one another.

Anna scooted back a little. She didn't want any of them hopping out of the pool and scratching her. When Lemondrop looked like she was trying to fly right at Anna, Anna jumped.

Reed laughed. "Look out! Chickens on the loose!"

"Be careful! Don't startle them." Kaya stroked Chicken Little's head with one finger. "I can't believe you get to take them home for the whole weekend, Anna."

The chicks couldn't stay alone at school on the weekends, so they went home with a different student every week. Anna didn't really want chick visitors at her house, but Kaya had been so sad when her parents told her it was against the rules of their apartment to bring the chicks home that Anna had volunteered instead. Then she invited Kaya over to help take care of them. It would be a chicken sleepover!

"Is this where the chickens are?" Anna's father knocked on the door of Anna's classroom. Anna's younger brother, Collin, stood next to him.

"Come on in," said Mr. Hoffman. "I'll go over all of the care instructions with you while the kids pack up the food and supplies."

Anna's father headed to Mr. Hoffman's desk, while Collin helped Anna, Reed, and Kaya put ten scoops of chicken feed into a plastic bag.

"I thought chickens ate bugs," said Collin.

"If they are allowed outside they will eat bugs," Kaya explained. "At school, we can't let

9

them wander around the playground, so we feed them special food instead."

When all the chicks' supplies were packed up, it was time for Reed to go home. Anna, Kaya, and Collin helped carry everything to the car. The chicks peeped and chirped in the backseat all the way to Anna's house. Kaya sat right next to them. She told the chicks what was happening so they wouldn't be too scared.

When they arrived home, the kids helped Mr. Fincher set everything up in the living room. The chicks weren't old enough yet to live outside by themselves.

"I wish I could sleep over at your house for the whole weekend instead of for just one night." Kaya lay down on her stomach and propped herself up on her elbows so she could watch the chicks sleep.

"I wish you could sleep over for the whole weekend too," Anna said. That seemed like the kind of thing best friends would do. "We could do spin art, make a music video, and ride scooters."

Kaya shook her head. "But I only have seven days left with the chicks. I wouldn't want to be separated from them for a single minute."

"Oh," Anna whispered back. Kaya only wanted to sleep over because of the chicks. "Okay."

Anna sat down by Kaya's feet. She wanted to be best friends with Kaya. But she wasn't sure how to ask someone if they wanted to be best friends.

Kaya folded her arms, rested her cheek against her hands, and watched the chickens'

fluff rustle gently as they slept. Her voice was soft and dreamy, like she was as sleepy as the chicks. "I wish they could stay at your house forever. If I can't have my own pet, at least then I could have a friend with a pet."

Anna made a wish too. She wished Kaya wanted a B-E-S-T friend with a pet.

BACKYARD
CHICKENS

The next morning Anna woke up when something fuzzy tickled her ear. She shrieked and tried to swat it away. For a second Anna thought a chick had escaped the brooder and was attacking her. Y-I-K-E-S! She never should have let Kaya convince her to sleep on the living room floor!

"Be gentle!" Kaya exclaimed. "Fluff wants to tell you a secret."

Anna slowly sat up and saw Kaya cupping Fluff in her hands. So she wasn't dreaming. A chick really had been tickling her ear.

"I woke up super early," Kaya said. "I couldn't wait to play with the chicks."

"What should we do today?" Anna asked. She thought about all the colored string in her art supplies box. Maybe they could make BFF bracelets.

"Let's take the chicks in your backyard," Kaya suggested. "They will love running around in the grass."

"Oh," Anna said. "Okay."

"What are you girls doing up so early?" Anna's father stood in the doorway of the living room. His hair was messy and he was wearing his bathrobe. "Don't you know it's Saturday?"

"We want to take the chicks outside," Anna told him.

"How about a little breakfast first?"

Kaya put Fluff back in the brooder and the girls followed Mr. Fincher into the kitchen, where they found all the ingredients for waffles on the counter. Mr. Fincher gave them a copy of the recipe and told them they were in charge of the batter.

"Cool." Kaya put on the green apron lying on the counter.

"Do you like to cook a lot?" Anna asked Kaya, as she put on a red apron. Maybe she could get Kaya her own baking set and an apron.

"Sure, I guess," Kaya said.

That didn't sound too enthusiastic.

"So, Kaya," Anna's father said as he plugged in the waffle iron, "Anna tells me it's almost your birthday."

"Uh-huh," Kaya said, scooping a cup of flour into the mixing bowl. "On Friday."

"Are you hoping for any special presents this year?" he asked.

Anna perked up her ears. Maybe Kaya would tell her dad what she wanted.

Kaya cracked an egg in the bowl and shrugged. "I can't think of anything special! I like *everything*."

Anna tried to hide her sigh. She carefully

measured a teaspoon of vanilla into the bowl. Kaya's answer wasn't any help at all.

After Anna and Kaya finished adding the rest of the ingredients, they took turns stirring the batter. Then they got dressed while Anna's father cooked the waffles. After breakfast, Reed and their friend Bailey from the Friendship Garden came over, and so did Collin's friend Jax.

In the backyard, they put together a baby gate that Anna's parents had kept from when she and Collin were little. Then they wrapped the gate around a small wooden playhouse. Anna and Collin were too big for it now, but the chicks fit perfectly. Anna, Kaya, Reed, Bailey, Collin, and Jax all stood inside the fence watching as the chicks pecked the dirt.

"Look!" Kaya beamed. "They love being outside."

"Do you think they're eating bugs?" Collin squatted next to Lemondrop and tried to watch his beak carefully.

"Fluff's trying to eat rocks," Reed said.

Reed pointed at Fluff, who was trying to pick up a pebble the size of a marble with her beak. It kept falling back down.

Kaya sighed. "I can't believe we have to say good-bye to them." She kneeled down near the playhouse and stuck her head inside. "Peep, peep," she said softly to the chicks.

"I got Kaya a T-shirt with a picture of the baby chicks on it for her birthday," Bailey whispered to Anna. "So she'll always remember them. My mom helped me take the picture last week after school, and then

we got it printed on a shirt!"

"She'll love it!" Anna told Bailey. Then she felt a funny flutter in her chest. She was happy that Kaya would have a baby chick T-shirt. She knew Kaya really would love it. But *she* wanted to be the one to give Kaya her favorite present. Why hadn't she thought of a baby chick T-shirt?

"I got her a bunch of wind-up chicks," Reed said in a low voice. He kept his eyes on Kaya to make sure she was still talking to the chicks. "I know they aren't real, but she can pretend they are pets."

"She's really good at pretending she has pets," Bailey told him. "I bet she'll name them Fluff, Feather, Lemondrop, and Chicken Little."

Kaya had more toy animals than anyone else Anna knew. Anna hadn't realized she would want even more. Now it was too late. She couldn't get toy chicks for Kaya if Reed already got them.

"What are you going to get for Kaya?" Bailey asked Anna.

Reed and Bailey looked at Anna expectantly. Anna didn't want to tell them she didn't know yet. What kind of friend can't even think up a birthday present?

Kaya pulled her head out of the tiny house. "What are you guys talking about?" she asked.

"Birthday presents," Reed said. "Anna was just about to tell us what she got you!"

"I can't tell you," Anna said, biting her lip. "It's a surprise."

Kaya's eyebrows went up. "I like surprises," she said.

"Well you'll love this one," said Anna. "It's

going to be the best birthday present ever."

"Whoa!" said Reed. "What'd you get her? A roller coaster or something?"

"I know!" said Bailey excitedly. "It's a pony!"

Anna gulped. Her stomach swayed back and forth. A roller coaster? A pony? She couldn't get Kaya anything like that. But she wanted to make sure Kaya was extra excited. "Even better," she promised.

"Whatever it is, I'm sure I'll like it." Kaya smiled at Anna. "Because it's from you!"

Anna nodded, but she didn't really believe Kaya. What if she got Kaya something she hated, like a jar of mayonnaise? If Anna wanted Kaya to be her best friend, she'd have to give Kaya the best present ever.

Now she just had to figure out what that was.

MORE CHICKENS?

Sunday mornings were Anna's favorite mornings. Most days, Anna's mother worked as a chef at a fancy restaurant. But on Sundays her restaurant was closed until dinnertime, so Anna's family always did something together on Sunday mornings. Every week it was different. Anna called it their Family Mystery Morning. Her parents usually planned the activity and then Collin and Anna would guess what it was.

"Will we be going in an airplane?" Collin asked Mr. and Mrs. Fincher as they all put on their shoes.

"No," said Anna's mom. "We'll be using our feet for transportation, so wear your sneakers."

"Will we be outside?" Anna asked her parents as they opened the door. Anna took one last peek to make sure the chicks were safe in their brooder, then she followed her parents.

Over the sound of cars honking in the distance, Anna also heard birds chirping. It was a sound she hadn't heard in months. It was almost the end of April, and spring weather had *finally* come to Chicago. The city even smelled like fresh dirt and grass. Of course that was mixed with the smells of car exhaust, coffee, and bread from the bakery down the street.

"We will start outside, because we are going to walk about ten blocks to get where we are going," said Anna's father, leading them all down the sidewalk. "Then when we arrive, we'll sit inside."

"Will there be toys?" Collin asked.

Mrs. Fincher shook her head. "Not unless we bring our own."

Anna thought she might know. "Will there be food?" she asked.

"Oh yeah," said her father. "There will definitely be food."

"Are we going out for brunch?" Anna guessed.

"Ding, ding, ding!" Anna's father touched his nose and pointed at Anna. That was his goofy way of saying she was right.

"Yes!" Collin pumped his fist. "I'm getting pancakes."

Anna's family stopped at a corner and waited for the signal to change so they could cross the street. There were lots of kids walking around—more than Anna usually saw on the busy city streets of her neighborhood. For some reason, everywhere she looked Anna noticed pairs of girls huddled head-to-head. What was this, *Best Friends Day*?

When the light changed, Anna held her mother's hand and they crossed the street and then turned and cut through a park. "This is a brand-new restaurant," Anna's mother told them. "My friend Shonda just opened it. She's even growing some of the food herself."

"You should tell her about the Friendship Garden," Anna's father suggested as he patted Anna's head.

"I will," Anna said. "Do you think Shonda will let us see her garden?"

"She'll give you the grand tour!" Anna's mother said.

Anna's family exited the park and crossed one more street. "This is it." Anna's mother pointed to a colorful sign that said GREENS, EGGS, & HAM.

When they entered the restaurant, a crowd of people stood waiting for tables, but when Anna's mother gave her name at the hostess stand, Anna's family was seated right away.

"Shonda can't wait to see you," the hostess said. "She'll be out to say hi whenever she catches a break in the kitchen."

Anna's father picked up his menu and began to hum as he read all the choices. "I don't know how I'm going to be able to decide."

Anna didn't either. Everywhere she looked she saw scrumptious food. A mixed-berry yogurt parfait to her right, a stack of crunchy banana French toast to her left. Y-U-M!

"I'm going to order the Where the Wild Mushrooms Are omelet," Anna said.

"I'm going to get Winnie the Pancake," Collin announced. "It comes with chocolate chip eyes."

Forty-five minutes later, all four Finchers leaned back from the table with full bellies and full smiles.

"Those were the best eggs I've ever had," said Anna's father. "I have to know how Shonda makes them taste so fresh."

"I can't take any credit!"

Anna turned around and saw a beautiful woman with dark, smooth skin and a round, strong body. She wore a black-and-white striped apron. "The chickens are in charge of the eggs."

Collin's jaw dropped. "You have *chickens* cooking your food?"

Shonda laughed, and her eyes sparkled. "No. I do the cooking. The chickens do the laying!"

"You're raising chickens!" Anna's mother exclaimed. "Will we get to see them on the tour?"

Shonda stepped back and gestured to a door near the rear of the dining area. "Right this way."

More chickens? Anna couldn't believe it. Chickens seemed to be everywhere this weekend. Maybe it was Best Friends Day *and* Chicken Day.

Anna followed her family and Shonda into an empty lot that reminded Anna a little bit of Shoots and Leaves, the community garden where the Friendship Garden grew their vegetables. On one side of the lot were several raised garden beds. Most of them were covered with white plastic domes.

Shonda pointed to one of the domes and explained, "These help me grow vegetables even in winter. They let sunlight in, but keep the cold out. Of course we also have a real greenhouse." Shonda pointed to a little glass building filled with plants. "Gotta have tomatoes and spinach year-round."

Anna's heart made a happy pitter-patter. She never knew vegetables could grow during the winter. C-O-O-L. Maybe Shonda could teach the Friendship Garden about those white domes the next time the weather got cold. She would ask Mr. Hoffman if they could try it. Mr. Hoffman was not only their teacher but also the grown-up in charge of the Friendship Garden.

At the back of the lot Anna saw another little house. This one was made out of wood, not glass, and it was raised up on stilts. The house, along with a patch of grass and shrubbery, was surrounded by a wire fence. Behind the fence roamed lots and lots and lots of chickens.

"That looks just like the playhouse in our backyard," Collin said, pointing to the chicken coop. "Only it's got legs."

Shonda laughed. "That keeps critters from living under the coop. It also makes a nice shady spot for the chickens to rest on hot days. But mostly it makes it easy for me to reach the eggs."

Anna watched a chicken walk up the ramp and into the chicken coop. The coop was painted a rainbow of colors, with green walls, a blue roof, pink shutters, and an orange door. It was too bad she couldn't get Kaya a chicken coop to decorate for her birthday. It would combine both of Kaya's favorite things, art *and* animals.

But Kaya lived in an apartment. She didn't have a backyard for a chicken coop and her parents wouldn't let her have pets anyway.

"Would anyone like to collect some eggs?" Shonda asked, opening the gate to the chicken yard.

Anna's parents and Collin all walked inside, but Anna stayed put. Collin scattered seeds on the ground and all the chickens in the yard raced over to him, clucking and bobbing their necks. It almost looked like they were dancing as they pecked all over the ground. Anna's father tried to get out of their way, but one of the chickens pecked his shoelace and wouldn't let go. He had to hop on one foot to get away. Anna laughed.

Those chickens sure looked happy. Anna thought it would be fun if there was a coop next to the Friendship Garden. She could watch the chickens while she planted. And she wouldn't have to get too close to them.

Oh!

Suddenly Anna's eyes opened wide and a thought pecked at her brain like a hungry chick. She had an I-D-E-A.

What if there really *was* a coop next to the Friendship Garden? Maybe Anna could convince Mr. Hoffman to let them keep the baby chicks and raise them in Anna's old playhouse. Maybe Maria would let the Friendship Garden use some of the extra land in Shoots and Leaves to set up a chicken yard. Anna would talk to her father as soon as they got home. She'd need a grown-up to help her.

If Anna did all those things, then Kaya wouldn't have to say good-bye to the baby chicks. She'd get to paint a chicken coop and take care of chickens like they were her very own pets!

It really would be the best present ever!

THE BIG CHICKEN QUESTION

That Monday after school Anna, Kaya, Bailey, and Reed walked with Mr. Hoffman to Shoots and Leaves for their first spring visit to the Friendship Garden.

Anna couldn't wait. She wanted to start planting, but she also wanted to ask Mr. Hoffman about her chicken idea. She'd already asked her father, and they'd spent the evening researching how to build a coop. Now Anna just had to find a way to ask Mr. Hoffman without anyone overhearing. The idea *had* to stay a surprise for Kaya's birthday.

Mr. Hoffman set an easel up next to the Friendship Garden's plot. On the easel he wrote a list of all the things good gardeners do to prepare for a new planting season.

To Prepare a Garden for Spring:
1. Turn the soil
2. Add some compost
3. Pick your crops
4. Make a planting map

Today all the Friendship Gardeners were going to work on steps one and two. Mr. Hoffman grabbed a bunch of shovels and rakes

from the new Friendship Garden supply cabinet. Then he showed them how to flip the soil so it would be loose and crumbly. He passed out one tool to each student.

"Let's work over here," Kaya said to Anna, Reed, and Bailey. "Maybe Anna can make up a game for us while we work."

Anna loved making up games for her friends, but if she worked next to Kaya, Kaya might get suspicious when Anna snuck away to talk to Mr. Hoffman. Anna didn't want to have to lie. It was better if Kaya didn't ask any questions.

"You guys work over there," Anna said, taking a step away from her friends. "I'm going to turn the soil on the other side of the garden."

Kaya made a funny face. "Oh. Well we don't mind working on that side. We'll come with you." Kaya began to walk to the other side of the garden.

"No!" Anna spoke louder than she meant to, and felt bad when Kaya looked hurt. She tried to soften her words. "I just feel like gardening by myself today."

"Okay," Kaya said, but she still sounded confused. "We'll be right here if you change your mind."

"Yeah," Reed said. "Sometimes when I'm in a bad mood, being alone for a few minutes really helps. And taking some elephant breaths."

Anna wasn't in a bad mood, but she couldn't explain. She just smiled and took a deep breath like Reed suggested.

"Feel better," Bailey said.

Anna watched Kaya, Bailey, and Reed get to work scooping. Then Anna settled herself on the left side of the garden next to Simone, a fifth-grader whose mother was the president of Shoots and Leaves.

"Hi, Anna," Simone said when Anna

kneeled down next to her and began to till the dirt. "Why are you over here? Did you get in a fight with your friends?"

Anna shook her head. "I want to do something really cool for Kaya's birthday, but it has to do with the Friendship Garden too. And I don't want her to know."

Simone stopped digging and looked at Anna with one raised eyebrow. "*Mysterious!* So what's the big secret?"

Anna looked around to make sure no one could overhear their conversation, then she lowered her voice. "I can tell *you* because I'm going to have to ask your mom for permission. Maybe you could help me with that." Anna cupped her hands around her mouth and whispered her last sentence. "I want the Friendship Garden to raise chickens."

"Chick—" Simone started to shout, but Anna put her hand right over Simone's mouth. Didn't Simone remember this was T-O-P S-E-C-R-E-T?

Anna looked all around the garden, but everyone was still working. "That was a close call," Anna said. "We have to be quiet!"

Simone nodded. "Chickens would be the coolest thing ever!" she whispered. "And don't worry about my mom. She'll say yes if she thinks it's good for the garden members."

Just then Anna noticed Mr. Hoffman heading over to the shed where Maria worked.

"I'm going to ask the Big Chicken Question now," Anna said. She waited until Kaya, Bailey, and Reed were looking in the other direction, then she snuck over to the shed. Mr. Hoffman was talking with Maria and Mr. Eggers, another member of Shoots and Leaves.

"Hi, Anna!" Mr. Hoffman said.

Anna's heart began to tap against her chest. She thought it was what the inside of an egg must feel like when a chick was trying to get out. She wanted to ask her question, but what if Mr. Hoffman said no? Anna didn't even want to think about that.

"Shouldn't you be helping your friends?" Mr. Eggers frowned and pointed at the Friendship Garden. Mr. Eggers usually sounded pretty grumpy. "There's a lot of work to do in

a spring garden," he added. "They need you."

"I'll get back to work soon. I just have a question. Or maybe it's an idea," she said, looking back and forth between Mr. Hoffman and Maria. "For both of you."

Maria's eyes widened, but she smiled. "Go ahead. It seems that every time you have an idea something special happens."

"This weekend my family went to a restaurant that grows its own vegetables in a garden just like this one," Anna said.

"I read about that restaurant online!" Maria said. "I can't wait to try it."

"It was really tasty," Anna said. "My mom's friend Shonda runs it. Shonda also raises chickens behind the restaurant, right in her garden."

"Cool!" said Mr. Hoffman.

"I used to raise chickens when I was a boy," Mr. Eggers said. "Didn't think anyone cared about that sort of thing nowadays."

"Well I care," Anna said. She took another elephant breath. "So I was thinking, maybe the Friendship Garden could keep the baby chicks from our class, and we could raise them right here."

"Whoa!" said Maria. "Chickens?"

"I never knew you liked the chicks so much," said Mr. Hoffman. "You always seemed a little afraid of them."

Anna felt her cheeks get warm and she looked at the dirt. "I am a little," she confessed. "But Kaya loves them. She would be so happy if she got to keep taking care of them and playing with them."

Anna snuck a peek over at Kaya to make

sure she was still busy. She was.

"I think lots of other kids would love to help take care of the chicks too," Anna added. Then she remembered Simone's advice. "And we could share the eggs with the members of Shoots and Leaves!"

Maria folded her arms across her chest. "Well I would say that chicks are a big responsibility, but you've already proven you can handle those. The Friendship Garden takes care of its plot better than some of the grown-ups around here.

"I've actually looked into raising chickens before, and if we get rid of the rickety old supply shed, there would be plenty of space at the back of the garden." Maria nodded at Mr. Hoffman. "It's okay with me if it's okay with you."

Anna's chest felt like it was about to explode. She couldn't believe Maria was saying yes. She turned to Mr. Hoffman. He wasn't smiling though. He was scratching his head.

"I'm not sure, Anna. It takes a lot of supplies to raise chickens. Things that we don't have in our classroom. For example, baby chicks can live in a brooder, but bigger chickens need to live in a—"

"Coop!" Anna finished Mr. Hoffman's sentence. "My family has an old playhouse that we can donate. We just need to raise it up on stilts, add a ramp, cover the windows with chicken wire, and make a few more changes. Shonda already e-mailed my dad the instructions for how to do it!"

"Mr. Eggers knows a lot about carpentry too," Maria added.

Mr. Eggers nodded. "I suppose I could help."

"That's great," Mr. Hoffman said, "but we'll need more than just that. What about a fence, and food? We'll have to think about keeping the chicks warm through the winter. This is a much bigger responsibility than a garden."

"I know." Anna nodded solemnly. "I looked it up on the Internet with my dad and lots of people raise chickens in Chicago. I know what to do."

Mr. Hoffman smiled. "It would be pretty neat, wouldn't it?" He looked up as if he were thinking, then smiled. "Okay."

Anna was so relieved, her eyes got watery. "Thank you!"

She quickly ran back to the Friendship Garden and told Simone the good news.

Simone squealed and hugged Anna tightly. From across the garden Kaya stood up. She gave Anna a questioning look and mouthed the words, "What happened?"

Anna shook her head and mouthed back, "Nothing."

Kaya pursed her lips like she didn't believe what Anna was saying, but Anna turned around. She grabbed her rake and began flipping the dirt again. She didn't want anything to spoil the surprise. When Kaya realized she'd be able to take care of the chickens forever, she was going to think Anna was the best friend in the world!

CHAPTER 5

CHICKEN PARTY

On Tuesday morning Mr. Hoffman asked if anyone would like to stay in at recess and plan the chicks' good-bye party.

Kaya's hand shot up faster than a rocket ship.

Mr. Hoffman laughed. "Okay, Kaya. Anyone else?"

Kaya looked at Anna and raised her eyebrows. Anna thought it might be hard to keep her secret and plan a good-bye party at the same time, but Kaya clasped her hands together and mouthed the word "Please."

Anna raised her hand. So did Bailey.

"Great! Two more helpers," Mr. Hoffman said.

When the bell rang for recess, most of Anna's class went outside, but Anna, Kaya, and Bailey sat by the chickens in Chicken School. Kaya brought her notebook and her colored pencils.

First Kaya and Bailey lifted all the chickens out of the brooder so that the chickens could run around the pool. Then Kaya opened her notebook and wrote *Chicken Party* at the top of the page in orange pencil.

"I have so many ideas," she said. "I found a recipe online for yummy chicken treats.

Everyone in our class could make one for the chickens as a going away present."

"That sounds good," Bailey said, and Kaya wrote *Make Chicken Treats* in her notebook.

Anna smiled softly to herself. The Friendship Garden could feed the treats to the chickens. Kaya would be so surprised.

"What's so funny?" Kaya asked Anna.

"Nothing!" Anna shook her head and tried to stop smiling.

"We should also get our pictures taken with the chickens. We could set up a photo booth next to Chicken School so everyone in the class can have a turn," Bailey suggested.

"Great idea!" Kaya wrote *Chicken Pictures* in her notebook. "What about you, Anna? Do you have any ideas?"

"Um . . ." All she could think about was how

excited Kaya would be when she realized the chickens weren't really going anywhere. She shrugged. "I can't really think of anything."

Kaya frowned. "That's okay. I know you don't like them very much."

"I like them," Anna said, but she jumped when one of the chicks flapped its wings in her direction.

"I know a really cute art project we could do with cotton balls and pipe cleaners," Bailey suggested. "Then we could all make our own baby chicks to take home."

"I love it," Kaya said, writing down *Make Baby Chicks*. She looked at Anna again. "Do you have any ideas yet?"

Anna shrugged. "Sorry. I don't."

Kaya wrinkled her eyebrows. She looked at Anna for a long time. Anna tried to smile, but she felt guilty. She didn't want to make Kaya upset by not helping with the party, but it would all be worth it when Anna revealed the surprise.

Just then Mr. Hoffman came back in the room. "Okay, girls, recess is nearly over. Please put the chicks back in the brooder, and leave a copy of your party ideas on my desk so I can get the supplies you need."

"Okay," Kaya said as she picked up Lemondrop and Feather. She put them in the brooder with Chicken Little. "Do you guys want to come over after school tomorrow to make the decorations?" she asked Bailey and Anna as they walked back to their desks.

"Sure," said Bailey.

It did sound like fun, but Anna was busy. Mr. Eggers had called Anna's father last night

63

and made plans to come over to Anna's house with wood and tools. They were going to turn her playhouse into a chicken coop.

"I can't," Anna told them. She made a sad face.

"Why not?" Kaya asked.

Anna's thoughts flapped around her brain like a baby chick playing in a little pool. What should she say? She couldn't tell Kaya the truth.

Anna blurted the first thing that popped into her head. "My dad and I are going to try a new recipe."

"Yum! What for?" Bailey asked.

"Um . . ." Anna's mind went blank. Her eyes darted around the classroom. Chicken Little scratched her feet on the bottom of the wading pool. "Chicken fingers!" Anna finally said, smiling because she'd thought of something.

Kaya pointed at the chicks, then put her hands on her hips. "Shh! Don't say that in front of them!"

Anna put her hand over her mouth. "Oops. I didn't mean . . . Sorry!"

Kaya shook her head and frowned. She looked at Anna with squinty eyes, like Anna was a stranger Kaya didn't recognize.

Anna sat down at her desk. She knew Kaya felt a little upset right now, but that would all change when she found out about the surprise. Anna only had to keep her secret for a few more days. Then Kaya would know she really was a good friend.

CHAPTER 6

CHICKEN FINGERS?

On Wednesday after school, Anna met her father by the flagpole. He was standing with Daisy, Kaya's *abuela*. *Abuela* was Spanish for grandmother. Kaya, Bailey, and Reed were all getting picked up by Daisy because Daisy watched Kaya after school.

"Hi, Daisy!" Anna said. "Hi, Dad."

"Hey, kiddos." Anna's father gave everyone high-fives.

"Hi, Mr. F," Reed said. "Kaya told me about your new recipe. If you finish early enough, do you think you could bring some chicken fingers to Kaya's house? I like mine with ranch dressing."

Anna's father wrinkled up the side of his nose in confusion. "Chicken fingers?" he asked.

Oh no! Anna didn't want her friends to realize she'd made up the chicken fingers story.

"I don't think we'll be finished in time," Anna said quickly, before her father could respond. "Chicken fingers take forever."

Now Mr. Fincher gave Anna his confused look. "*Chicken fingers?*" he asked again.

Anna tried to give her father a supersecret sign. She squinted one eye at him and nodded her head. "Yeah, remember? We're trying a new recipe today, right?"

Mr. Fincher didn't understand. "What about Mr. Eg—" he started to say.

Anna cut him off. "Oh, Mr. Egg? My new plant?! I'll water him later."

Now it was Kaya and Bailey's turn to look confused. And suspicious. They *knew* she didn't have a new plant. Anna tugged on her father's hand. It was time to go.

"Are you sure you don't want to join us, *niña*?" Daisy tilted her head as she gave Anna a thoughtful look. "I know Kaya would be *muy feliz* if you came."

Anna looked at Kaya. Kaya looked at the ground.

Anna felt a little prickle of guilt in her chest. She knew it would make Kaya happy if she helped with the Chicken Party, but it would make Kaya even happier if the Friend-ship Garden could keep the chickens.

"I can't." Anna bit her bottom lip. "Sorry."

She said good-bye to Kaya, Bailey, and Reed, and she and her father walked away.

"What was that about?" he asked her. "Are you upset with your friends?"

"No." Anna wasn't upset with her friends, but she did feel upset. Keeping a secret was harder than she thought. "Kaya doesn't know about the chickens. Nobody does. I want it to be a big surprise for her birthday."

"Hmm," said her father. "That's too bad. We could have used some more helpers. Besides, it will be exciting no matter when she finds out, won't it?"

"But I don't want it to be plain old exciting,

I want it to be the *most exciting ever* for her birthday." Anna's chest swelled with the feeling. *Nothing* could be better than giving her friend the most perfect present.

"Hmm," said her father. He didn't look like he agreed.

When Mr. Eggers arrived a little later, Anna realized her father was right about one thing. It would have been nice to have more helpers.

Mr. Fincher spread out the chicken coop plans Shonda had e-mailed, and Anna helped the grown-ups gather supplies.

First they had to unload a whole bunch of wood. Anna never knew wood could be so H-E-A-V-Y.

"Where did you get all this lumber?" Mr. Fincher asked.

"This is from the old Shoots and Leaves supply shed," Mr. Eggers replied. "Maria and I took it apart this morning. Half of the wood was rotting, but the other half was in great shape. I figured this would be the perfect use for it."

Turning a playhouse into a chicken coop took a lot of wood. First they attached a bar

across the top so the chickens could roost up high at night. Anna was in charge of sanding the wood smooth.

Next they built nesting boxes all along one wall where the chickens would lay their eggs. They made a little door above the nesting boxes, so Anna and her friends could collect the eggs without having to climb inside the coop. Anna was in charge of hammering.

When those jobs were finished, Anna, Mr. Eggers, and her father covered all the windows with screen and chicken wire. The wire would keep the chickens safe inside the coop at night.

By that time Anna was so tired she could barely lift her arms, but Mr. Eggers said, "Next we need to attach the stilts and then we need to build a chicken run."

"We have to do *more*?" Anna couldn't believe it.

Anna's father looked at his watch. "Not tonight. I've got to go pick up Collin at his friend's house."

"Why don't I come back tomorrow?" Mr. Eggers suggested. "We can try to finish up then."

"Are you sure you don't mind?" Anna's father asked.

"Yes," Anna agreed. "It's so nice of you to help."

"I don't mind," Mr. Eggers said. "I like to see kids taking care of real chickens instead of playing some chicken video game."

Anna smiled to herself. Underneath his grumpy face, Mr. Eggers was really kind.

"I don't understand why none of your friends

are helping with this chicken project," Mr. Eggers said as he packed his tools away in a red toolbox. "If we don't have more hands, I'm not sure we'll be able to get it all done by Friday."

Anna froze. She didn't want the secret to get out, but the chicken coop *had* to be done by Friday. That was Kaya's birthday! Maybe she could ask Reed and Bailey to help, but only if they promised not to tell Kaya.

"Okay," she said. "Tomorrow I'll have helpers."

That night Anna called Reed and then Bailey and told them about Kaya's surprise. Reed promised to help. But Bailey said, "What about the Friendship Garden? We were supposed to start planting tomorrow."

"Mr. Hoffman will understand if we miss. The chicken coop is for the Friendship Garden too." Anna filled her little red watering can so she could water her three plants, Chloe, Spike, and Fern, while she and Bailey spoke.

"Yeah, but what about Kaya?" Bailey asked. "Are you going to make her go to the Friendship Garden by herself tomorrow? What are we going to say when she asks why we're going home together without her?"

"She won't mind," Anna said, but even as she said it she wasn't sure if she believed it. Kaya might feel a little bad, but it would only be for one day. And she'd be so happy when she realized *why* they didn't go to the Friendship Garden.

Anna poured some water on Fern's soil. The water soaked in really quickly. Anna didn't realize she'd let her plant get so dry. "So will you help?"

"Okay," Bailey said. "But if Kaya asks me what we're doing, I'm going to tell her the truth."

"You can't!" Anna exclaimed. "And she won't ask. I'll think of a really good excuse."

After Anna hung up, she watered Chloe and Spike. Then she got into bed and tried to imagine what Kaya would say when she saw the Friendship Garden's new chicken coop on her birthday. She'd probably tell Anna she was the best friend in the whole entire world. Maybe she'd want to make BFF bracelets.

Anna smiled and fell asleep.

CHAPTER 7

CHICKENING OUT

The next day after school Kaya waited by Anna's cubby while Anna packed up her backpack, just like she always did on Friendship Garden days. All around them other kids were packing up to go home. Reed and Bailey had already left. They would meet Anna at the back door of the school so Kaya wouldn't see them all going home together.

"Daisy told me there would be baby seedlings waiting for us at the garden today," Kaya told Anna. "Plus Mr. Hoffman bought seed packets. It will be so cool to plant exactly what we want this year!"

"It sure will," Anna agreed. Each student in the Friendship Garden got to choose a couple of vegetables to plant. Anna had picked tiny grape tomatoes and sugar snap peas. She felt sad that she wasn't going to be able to help plant them today.

"Um, I have to tell you something," Anna said as she put her take-home folder in her backpack and zipped the zipper.

"What?" Kaya asked.

"I can't go to the garden today."

Kaya's face fell into a big frown. "But Daisy

made guacamole for our snack. Your favorite!"

Daisy's guacamole was the B-E-S-T. Anna's mouth watered just thinking about it. But they had to get that coop finished if they wanted to surprise Kaya on her birthday.

Anna's frown mirrored Kaya's. "I wish I could go," Anna said. "But I don't feel good." Anna patted her tummy and made a face. "I might be getting the flu."

"Oh no!" Kaya put her hand on Anna's forehead. "Do you want me to take you to the nurse? Or get you some water?"

Kaya was such a good friend. She really deserved the best birthday present ever. Anna felt terrible about lying and promised herself that she'd never do it again.

"That's okay," Anna said slowly. She tried

to make her voice sound as weak as possible. "I probably just need to rest. You go ahead. I don't want to make you late."

Kaya folded her arms across her chest. "I'm not leaving you if you don't feel good. I'll walk you outside."

Anna swallowed. She couldn't let Kaya walk her to the back door. Then she'd see Bailey and Reed and the whole surprise would be ruined! She'd have to let Kaya walk her to the front door, then Anna would need to run around the building to meet the others.

When Anna and Kaya walked out the front door, they could see Daisy and Mr. Hoffman waiting by the flagpole with the rest of the kids in the Friendship Garden. Mr. Hoffman waved them over, but Anna didn't want to go. He might ask her about the chicken coop!

Kaya studied the group. "Hey!" she said. "Where are Bailey and Reed? Did either of them say anything about missing today?"

"Oh no!" Anna smacked her palm against her forehead. "I just remembered my dad said he'd pick Collin up by the back door today. I'd better hurry or I might miss them."

Anna started walking away before Kaya could see her guilty face.

"Do you want me to walk with you?" Kaya called after her.

"No!" Anna didn't look back as she called out, "Have fun at the Friendship Garden. See ya tomorrow!"

Anna ran around the school to the back doors where her father, Collin, Bailey, and Reed were already walking toward her.

"Where were you?" Bailey asked.

"We were just coming to look for you," her father said.

"I thought you had forgotten to come home," Collin said.

Anna shook her head. "I was with Kaya," she explained. "It's complicated."

The group walked across the playground, heading for Anna's house, when they heard a voice call to Anna's father. "Dale!"

Anna looked to see who was calling, and realized it was Mr. Hoffman. He was standing on the other side of the playground with Daisy, Kaya, and the rest of the Friendship Garden!

"Quick!" Anna whispered to Bailey and Reed. "Hide!" She didn't want Kaya to see them all together.

Reed and Bailey crouched behind the nearest thing they could find: a twirly slide.

It didn't hide them very well. Anna could see both their feet sticking out at the bottom. She thought she saw Kaya staring at the bottom of the slide too.

"What are you doing over here?" Anna's father called back across the playground to Mr. Hoffman. "Isn't the Friendship Garden in the other direction?"

"We heard Anna wasn't feeling well. We wanted to make sure she found you." Mr. Hoffman shaded his eyes and looked right at Anna. "I can see that she did. Feel better, Anna!"

"Thanks," Anna called. She waved to everyone, and most of them waved back. Kaya didn't, though. Her arms were folded across her chest. She turned to Daisy and said something, and Daisy gave Anna a curious look. Then she rubbed Kaya's back as the

Friendship Garden group walked around the school toward Shoots and Leaves.

"Okay, you guys," Anna called to Reed and Bailey when they were gone. "You can come out now."

Reed ducked under the slide and asked, "Do you think Kaya saw us?"

Bailey walked around the other side and said, "I'm pretty sure she did."

"Why don't you want to invite her to help?" Mr. Fincher asked Anna. "The more helpers the better."

Anna pictured Kaya arriving at the Friendship Garden Friday afternoon after the Chicken Party. She thought of how Kaya's face would look when she realized she didn't have to say good-bye after all. And when she discovered that Anna had been the one to

make it all happen, she'd know Anna was her best friend.

But telling Kaya now would be like chickening out.

"Trust me," Anna said. "It will be more special this way."

When Anna and her friends arrived at her house, Mr. Eggers was waiting for them. He hadn't been kidding. They still had a lot of work to do!

They sawed and hammered and sanded until dinnertime, building the platform for the coop and the walls and roof for the chicken run. They still weren't finished when Bailey's mom and Reed's nanny came to pick them up.

"Don't worry," Mr. Eggers told Anna. "There isn't much left to do. Your father and I

can finish it tomorrow when we bring everything to Shoots and Leaves. By the time you
arrive there after school, the only thing missing will be the chickens."

Anna gave Mr. Eggers a hug. "Thank you!"

CHAPTER 8

CHICKEN DISASTER

When Anna arrived at school the next morning, she raced over to where Kaya was waiting in line for the bell to ring.

"Happy birthday!" she cheered, handing Kaya the card she'd made.

Kaya took the card and tucked it into her backpack without looking at it. Then she shrugged and turned away from Anna.

"Kaya?" Anna said, shuffling in a circle so that she could see her friend's face again. "Is everything okay?"

"I guess I don't feel well," Kaya said, then she went to stand at the back of the line, away from Anna.

Anna tried to follow her, but the bell rang and it was time to go inside.

All morning long Anna tried to talk to Kaya, but it wasn't easy to do. Their desks weren't close to each other, and Kaya had her nose buried in her work whenever Anna was nearby.

At lunchtime, Kaya sat next to Rosie and Jazmin, instead of with Anna like she usually did. At recess, she asked Rosie and Jazmin to help put up the decorations for the Chicken Party.

"I told you she'd be mad," Bailey said as they walked around the edge of the playground. "I think you should just tell her about the coop now."

"But we're so close." If Anna told her now, the whole surprise would be ruined. All that work keeping it a secret would be for nothing.

At the end of the day Anna's class had their Chicken Party. While most of the kids played Pin the Tailfeathers on the Chicken, Kaya sat in the corner, cuddling Lemondrop with a big frown on her face.

Anna sat next to Kaya. Lemondrop squawked at Anna, but Anna didn't scoot away, even though she wanted to.

"Are you sad about the chickens?" Anna asked.

Kaya let one finger trail down the back of

Lemondrop's head. "I guess," she answered.

"Well, I have a birthday surprise that will really cheer you up," Anna told her with a smile. "I'm going to show it to you at the Friendship Garden today."

Kaya shrugged and put Lemondrop back in the brooder. Then she picked up Chicken Little and started petting her back. "I'm not going today."

"What?" Anna felt like someone had just splashed cold water on her face. "But you *have* to go!" If Kaya didn't go, how would Anna show her the surprise?

"I already talked about it with Daisy," Kaya said. "I don't know if I want to do the Friendship Garden anymore. I used to spend a lot more time doing art projects. And I never get to see my cousins after school."

Anna's heart started pounding. How could her surprise have gone so badly? All she had wanted was to give Kaya a birthday present so special that Kaya would know how important their friendship was, but instead it seemed like Kaya didn't even want to be her friend anymore.

This was a D-I-S-A-S-T-E-R!

"Please come to the Friendship Garden." Anna clasped her hands together. "Please."

Kaya shrugged and nuzzled her cheek against Chicken Little. She didn't answer. Then the bell rang.

After school, Mr. Hoffman and the kids going to the Friendship Garden met by the flagpole as usual. Anna's eyes searched the crowd for Kaya, but she didn't see her anywhere. And Kaya definitely wasn't part of the group standing by the flagpole.

"Do you think she'll come?" Anna asked Bailey and Reed.

"I hope so," Bailey said, but she didn't sound too hopeful.

"I don't know," said Reed, shaking his head. "I heard her tell Jazmin that she was going to go to her cousin's house after school today."

"But she can't!" Anna put her head in her hands. There had to be a way to get Kaya to the Friendship Garden. Anna looked up and saw Kaya walking with Daisy by the fence. They were just about to leave the school property.

"Mr. Hoffman!" Anna cried. "Can I go talk to Kaya for a second?" Anna pointed across the schoolyard.

Mr. Hoffman looked at his watch. "You'll

have to be quick. It's almost time for us to start walking to Shoots and Leaves."

Anna ran as fast as she could. She reached Kaya and Daisy just as they had stepped onto the sidewalk in front of the school. "Kaya, wait!"

Kaya kept walking but Daisy stopped, so finally Kaya had to stop too. She turned around with her arms folded across her chest and an angry look on her face.

"Won't you stop at the Friendship Garden, just for a second?"

"What do you care?" Kaya asked. "All the other times I've gone this week you've either ignored me or made me go by myself."

Anna felt her cheeks blaze. She hadn't realized she had been making her friend so upset. Anna glanced at Daisy, who had taken a step backward but was watching the whole conversation. Anna wondered if Daisy agreed that she was a horrible friend.

"I'm so sorry," Anna said. "I didn't mean to ignore you. It was all for your birthday surprise. If you'll just come to the Friendship Garden, you'll see what I mean."

"I already know about the chicken coop," Kaya said. She didn't unfold her arms. And she didn't seem very excited.

"You do?" Anna shook her head. "How?"

"Daisy told me yesterday when you and

Bailey and Reed snuck off to work on it without me."

Anna looked at Daisy, who half-shrugged, half-smiled. "Mr. Eggers told me about your project. *Lo siento.* I'm sorry, but it was the best thing to do."

"She thought it would make me feel better if I knew what you were doing," Kaya explained. "But it didn't. It made me feel worse."

Anna swallowed, and a big lump of guilt stuck in her throat. "It did?"

Kaya nodded. "I felt like you guys were having more fun without me."

"I'm sorry," Anna told her. "I wanted to give you the most perfect birthday present in the whole wide world."

"Well it felt like you cared more about the present than you did about me," Kaya said sadly. "The thing I like best in the world is being with my friends."

Anna looked at the ground. Kaya was right. Instead of thinking about what Kaya would have liked best, Anna had been thinking about trying to give the best present. "Me too. I should have told you my plan and asked you to help when I realized how hard it was to keep the secret. But won't you come help us now? We need to paint the chicken coop and the chicken run, and I thought you could be in charge of the design."

Kaya's eyes looked up, and for a moment Anna felt hopeful. Kaya loved to paint. But then Kaya shook her head. "I already made plans to go to my cousin's house," she said. "You'll have to paint it without me."

Anna wished she could convince Kaya to

come for even a little bit, but Mr. Hoffman called to her. "Anna, time to go!"

Anna looked back and forth between Kaya and Mr. Hoffman. Mr. Hoffman waved his arm, calling her over. "I have to go," Anna said to Kaya. "But I'm really sorry. I guess I got carried away because I wanted my present to show you how much I like you." Anna took a deep breath. "You're my best friend."

Kaya didn't say anything. Anna's heart sank.

"Anna!" Mr. Hoffman called again, and Anna ran back to the group alone.

CHAPTER 9

THE FRIENDSHIP COOP

When the kids in the Friendship Garden arrived at Shoots and Leaves and saw the chicken coop, they were all as surprised as Anna had hoped Kaya would be!

"Is that a playground for babies?" Jax wanted to know.

"Are we going to grow vegetables in there?" asked Simone.

Mr. Hoffman turned to Anna. "Do you want to explain the Friendship Garden's new project to everyone?"

Anna shook her head. She didn't feel enthusiastic about the chickens anymore. It wouldn't be fun without Kaya.

"As some of you know, for the past two months, my class has been raising baby chicks. Now that they are too big to live in our classroom, we've decided to build them a home right here in Shoots and Leaves. The Friendship Garden will get to take care of them."

From all the excited murmurs and giggles around her, Anna could tell that everyone thought it was a great idea.

"Today," Mr. Hoffman continued, "in addition to finishing our spring planting, you can all take turns helping us paint the chicken coop."

"How are we going to paint it?" asked Reed.

"Like a barn," suggested one kid.

"Like a rainbow," suggested another.

"I think we should just paint it one color," said Simone. "Maybe yellow or green?"

Then everyone started shouting out ideas and opinions all at once.

Anna's heart sank even further. This was all so different from what she imagined. Kaya was the artist. *She* should be helping them decide what to paint.

"Wait!" Anna said. "Maybe we shouldn't paint it today."

"Aww." A bunch of kids groaned.

"I don't think we should wait to paint," someone said. "Then the chickens will have to wait to move in to their new home."

The voice sounded familiar, and Anna's chest swelled with hope. She looked up. Kaya!

Anna ran over to her. "I thought you weren't coming."

"Daisy convinced me that we could go to my cousin's later." Kaya smiled. "Besides, I really wanted to see the chicken coop."

Anna grabbed Kaya's hand and took her over to the run. "It's made out of the old playhouse in my backyard," she explained.

"It's great!" Kaya beamed. "The chickens will be so happy here. I'm going to come visit them every day."

"How do you think we should paint it?" Simone asked.

"I think each person should paint a picture of themselves, one next to the other, going all around the coop holding hands. That way the chickens will feel safe and protected."

"We could call it the Friendship Coop," Anna suggested.

"What does everyone think?" Mr. Hoffman asked.

Everyone liked the idea, so Mr. Hoffman asked Kaya to organize the painting. He said she could choose one person to be her helper. Anna looked at the ground. She wanted Kaya to pick her, but she didn't expect her to.

"I choose Anna," Kaya said. Anna's heart soared.

The two girls opened the gate of the chicken run and went inside to set up the jars of paints around the coop.

Anna had used all the money in her piggy bank to buy paints in lots of different colors.

"So what's your favorite part of the chicken coop?" Anna asked.

Kaya looked all over, at the windows with little shutters, at the big fenced-in run with its squeaky gate, then she looked at Anna. "I think my favorite thing is that I get to share it with my best friend."

Anna's smile was so big she thought it might stretch off her face. She squeezed Kaya's hand. That was definitely Anna's favorite thing too.

ACTIVITY: **MAKE YOUR OWN MINI COMPOST BIN**

When Anna and her friends prepare the garden for spring, an important step is adding compost to the soil. Compost is a mixture of food waste and dead plant materials that have decomposed into a crumbly brown substance that looks like soil. It is full of great nutrients for growing new plants.

You can make compost and use it to grow your own plants either in a planter or in a garden.

What you will need:

2-liter soda bottle

rubber band

marker

scissors

potting soil

fruit and vegetable scraps

dirt from outside

fertilizer (can buy at a nursery or
    garden center)

brown leaves collected from outside

What you will do:

First rinse out the bottle, screw the top back
on, then remove the label.

About one-third of the way down the bottle,
draw a line three-fourths of the way around
the bottle. (You can use a rubber band to help
you trace a straight line.) Now with the help of
a grown-up, use scissors to cut along the line.
Now you will have a sort of flip-top lid.

Next place a layer of soil in the bottom of
the bottle. Moisten the soil with water from

a spray bottle if it is dry. Add a thin layer of fruit and vegetable scraps, a thin layer of dirt, a tablespoon of fertilizer, and a layer of leaves. Continue adding layers until the bottle is almost full.

Tape the flip-top lid shut and place your bottle outside in a sunny location. If moisture condenses on the sides of the bottle, remove the top to let it dry out. If the contents look dry, add a squirt or two of water from a spray bottle.

Roll the bottle around every day to mix the contents. The compost is ready to use when it is brown and crumbly. This takes a month or so.

RECIPE: **WHERE THE WILD MUSHROOMS ARE OMELET**

(serves 2)

Ingredients:

4 eggs

1 tbsp milk or cream

½ cup chopped mushrooms (you can use a mix of chanterelle, shitake, portabella, or any of your favorite mushrooms)

¼ cup shredded mozzarella

1 tbsp chopped parsley

1 tbsp olive oil

salt and pepper

Instructions:

1. Heat the olive oil in a small nonstick frying

pan. Tip in the mushrooms and fry over a high heat, stirring occasionally for 2–3 minutes until golden. Lift out of the pan and into a bowl. Mix with the cheese and parsley.

2. In a small bowl, mix the eggs and milk.

3. Pour the egg mix into the frying pan and cook over medium–high heat. Cook for 1 minute or until set to your liking, swirling with a fork now and again.

4. Spoon the mushroom mix over one half of the omelet. Using a spatula, flip the omelet over to cover the mushrooms. Cook for a few moments more, then lift onto a plate. Season with salt and pepper.

Read on for more
FRIENDSHIP GARDEN
adventures in *Sweet Peas and Honeybees!*

CHAPTER 1

S-U-M-M-E-R!

Little glimmers of sunlight sparkled in Anna Fincher's window, and one sunny beam warmed her cheek. Anna sat up in bed and smiled at the green leaves of the oak tree fluttering outside her bedroom window. She tilted her head and listened to the sweet coo of a mourning dove. There was only one word that could describe such a perfect day: S-U-M-M-E-R!

Anna hopped out of bed and got dressed in the special outfit she laid out the night before. Shorts and a light tee shirt to keep herself cool, a wide brimmed hat to keep the sun off her face, and thick socks with sturdy gardening boots. Anna couldn't wait to spend all day in the Friendship Garden.

During the school year, Anna and her friends visited the garden several times a week as part of an after-school gardening club. Now that it was summer, Anna's teacher, Mr. Hoffman, was leading a Friendship Garden summer program called Friends, Fun, and Flowers. For two whole weeks, Anna and her friends would get to hang out in the garden all day. Well, not really all day, since there would be field trips and other activities in addition to gardening.

Anna hurried to the kitchen for breakfast.

"Good morning, Anna Banana!" Anna's father was already in the kitchen. He was the main cook at home, because Anna's mother was the head chef at a fancy restaurant. Mr. Fincher spooned a large dollop of yogurt into a blue bowl. "This morning I will be serving make-your-own yogurt bowls with homemade granola."

Anna took her bowl to the table and spooned sliced bananas, blueberries, granola, and a drizzle of honey onto her yogurt as Anna's mother shuffled into the kitchen in her pajamas. Anna's younger brother, Collin, walked in behind her carrying a butterfly net and a magnifying glass. Collin swung the net around and then plunked it down right on Anna's head.

"Gotcha!" he shouted.

Anna pulled the net from her hair. "I'm not a bug, Collin," she reminded him, even though that seemed obvious to her.

"I know," Collin said. "I was just practicing."

Anna took a deep breath and tried not to feel annoyed as Collin laid down his net. When everyone was at the table, Anna's mom wrapped both hands around her coffee mug and said, "Are you two ready for camp?"

Anna nodded as she licked yogurt and honey from the back of her spoon. "I can't wait! Maria gave the Friendship Garden an extra plot so we can grow rosebushes and fancy flowers!"

Collin looked at Anna's bowl, then added all the same toppings to his yogurt as Anna. "I can't wait too," Collin said taking a mouthful of yogurt. He finished chewing, then added. "Bugs, Bugs, Bugs is going to be even better than first grade. The website said that a real entomologist is going to talk to us. That's a person who studies bugs!"

Collin wriggled his fingers, then crawled them up Anna's arm. A shiver ran down her spine. She knew bugs could be important for the garden, but she didn't like to get too close to them.

Anna liked her little brother, but sometimes it seemed like all he thought about was bugs—and his favorite bug was bugging Anna. She was glad they would each be doing their own activity for the summer.

"I hope I find an Eastern Tiger Swallowtail today!" Collin said.

Anna's parents gave each other a look,

then her father sighed. "Collin, we have to tell you something that might be a little disappointing."

Collin tilted his head and looked at his father through the magnifying glass. "What?" he asked.

"We found out last night that not enough kids signed up for Bugs, Bugs, Bugs," Anna's mother said. "They had to cancel the class."

"But," Anna's father held up one finger, "because bugs and gardens naturally go together, they've decided to combine the classes."

Anna's parents watched Collin with concerned expressions. "What do you think?" Anna's mom asked.

Collin took another bite of granola and shrugged while he chewed. "Okay," he finally said. "Sounds good. Now Anna and I can be partners if we need partners for something."

Anna's parents sat back in their chairs, both smiling with relief. "Anna's a great partner," said her father. "I'm glad you're not too disappointed."

Anna ate another bite of yogurt to hide her frown. Anna wasn't glad that Collin was joining her gardening class. And she wasn't glad that gardening had turned into gardening and bugs. She wanted to learn about marigolds and morning glories, not about creepy-crawlies. And she wanted to hang out with her friends, not with her brother. Suddenly Anna's perfect summer day felt a lot less perfect.